Arma

Written by Lee-Ann Wright

Rigby

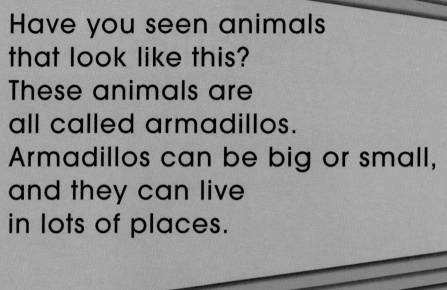

Have you seen animals
that look like this?
These animals are
all called armadillos.
Armadillos can be big or small,
and they can live
in lots of places.

Look at the armadillo's body.
An armadillo has scales
on its body.
The scales are very hard.
They help keep
the armadillo safe.

scales

hair

Some armadillos have hair
on their bodies, too.

Armadillos cannot see very well,
but they are good at smelling.
They smell the ground
looking for food.
They eat ants and
other little insects.

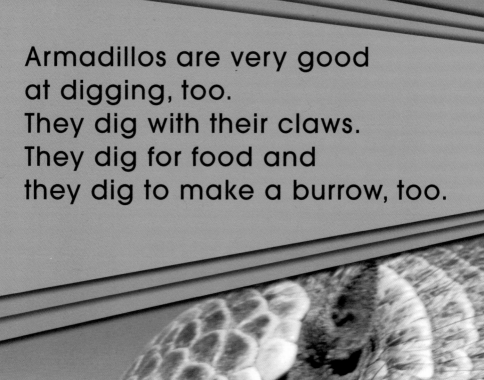

Armadillos are very good
at digging, too.
They dig with their claws.
They dig for food and
they dig to make a burrow, too.

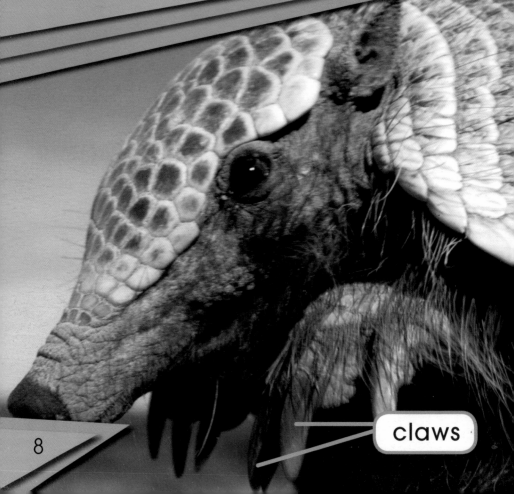

claws

Armadillos live in holes called burrows.

A mother armadillo keeps
her baby in a burrow.
A baby armadillo does not have
hard scales like its mother.
The scales will get hard when
the baby gets bigger.

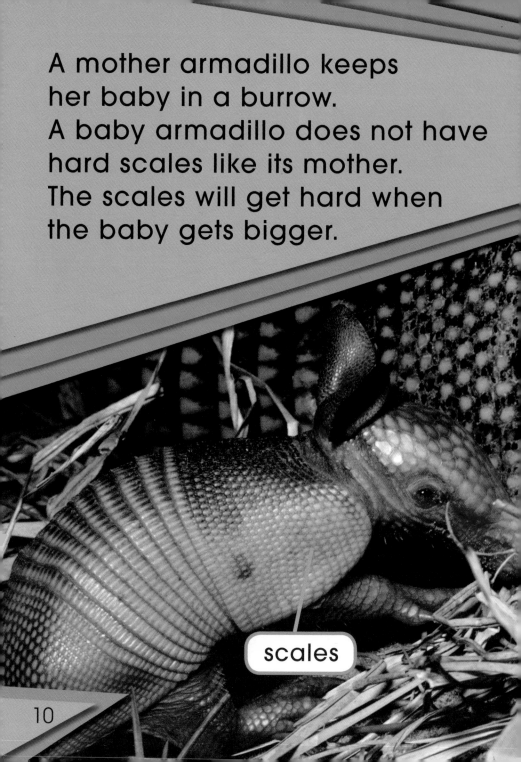

scales

When an armadillo is scared,
it can run away, or it can run
into its burrow.
Some armadillos will stay
very still, and some armadillos
will jump up into the air!

burrow

This armadillo is smart.
When there is danger,
it rolls into a ball.
When the danger is gone,
the armadillo will open up again.

Index

Guide Notes

Title: Armadillos
Stage: Early (4) – Green

Genre: Nonfiction
Approach: Guided Reading
Processes: Thinking Critically, Exploring Language, Processing Information
Written and Visual Focus: Photographs (static images), Index, Labels, Caption, Flow Chart

---

THINKING CRITICALLY
(sample questions)

- Look at the front cover and the title. Ask the children what they know about armadillos.
- Look at the title and read it to the children.
- Focus the children's attention on the index. Ask: "What are you going to find out about in this book?"
- If you want to find out how an armadillo digs, what page would you look on?
- If you want to find out what an armadillo does when it is in danger, what pages would you look on?
- Look at pages 4 and 5. How do you think scales can help keep the armadillo safe?
- Look at page 14. How do you think rolling into a ball could help the armadillo when danger is near?

EXPLORING LANGUAGE

Terminology
Title, cover, photographs, author, photographers

Vocabulary
Interest words: armadillo, scales, burrow
High-frequency words: called, or, keep, still, gone
Positional words: in, on, into, up
Compound words: into, cannot

Print Conventions
Capital letter for sentence beginnings, periods, commas, exclamation mark, question mark, possessive apostrophe